This book belongs to ...

....

Tips for Talking and Reading Together

Stories are an enjoyable and reassuring way of introducing children to new experiences.

Before you read the story:

- Talk about the title and the picture on the cover. Ask your child what they think the story might be about.
- Talk about how an optician might test your eyes. Does your child wear glasses? Has your child ever been to the optician?

Read the story with your child. After you have read the story:

- Discuss the Talk About ideas on page 27.
- Talk about how to look after your eyes on pages 28–29 and talk about why it is important to look after your eyes.
- Do the fun activity on page 30.

Have fun!

Find the 10 different fruits hidden in the pictures.

For more hints and tips on helping your child become a successful and enthusiastic reader look at our website **www.oxfordowl.co.uk.**

Going to the Optician

Written by Roderick Hunt and Annemarie Young

Illustrated by Alex Brychta

OXFORD

UNIVERSITY PRESS

Anna had come to stay for a few days. Kipper and
Anna did a drawing, then Kipper read his book with Mum.

"That's very good, Kipper," said Mum. "Now,
I'm going to make an extra big pizza."

"Get me the tomato puree out of the cupboard, please," said Mum.

"Here it is," said Kipper.

The pizza was ready, so they all took a slice.

"This tastes like strawberry and tomato," said Chip.
"Strawmato!"

"Yuk, you used strawberry sauce instead of tomato puree," said Biff.

"They do look alike," said Mum. "Didn't you notice either, Kipper?"

"The label looked a bit fuzzy," said Kipper. "It's like at school when I look at the board. And my head aches sometimes too."

"Then we'd both better have our eyes tested," said Mum.
"We might get glasses like Anna," said Kipper.

So the next day Mum, Kipper and Anna went to
the optician.

"I'm Alison," said the optician. "I'm just going to check
your eyes."

"I'm going to make everything blurry, then I'll shine a light into your eyes," said Alison. "Keep looking at the light in the mirror."

"Show me the letter that you can see in the mirror," said Alison.

Kipper pointed to the letter on the card.

"What can you see through these funny glasses?" said Alison.

"Which lens is better, one or two?"

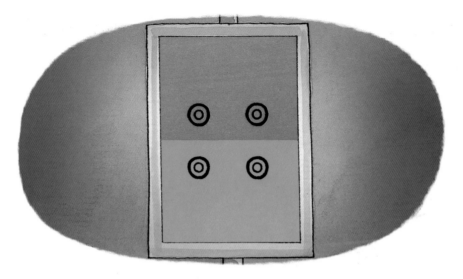

"Which circles look darker, the red or the green?"

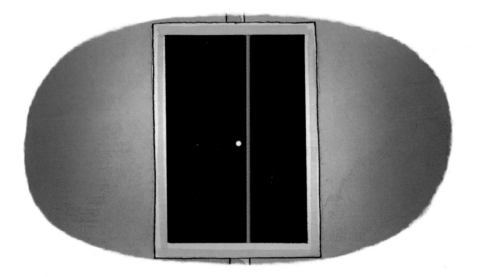

"Which side of the light is the line? Or is it in the middle?"

"You're doing very well, Kipper," said the optician.
"Now, I'm going to move this stick closer and closer.
Tell me when you see two clowns."

Alison gave Kipper a book. "Look at this page," she said.

"Ah," said the optician. "I know why the board at school looks fuzzy."

"Your eyes are fine, Kipper. You just need to hold the book further away when you're reading," said Alison, "and sit up straight."

"If you hold the book too close, your eyes get used to it. Then things further away look fuzzy. Like the board at school."

Kipper told everyone about the eye test. "It was fun," he said. "I just have to hold my book further away when I'm reading."

Dad read them a book about eyes.

"I wish I could see in the dark like owls and cats," said Kipper.

"Then eat your carrots!" said Dad.

"How about carrot cake?" said Kipper.

"Good idea," said Dad. "I'll make one. I've got a new recipe to try."

Dad's carrot cake was ready to bake. "Gas mark 8 and it will be ready in 2 hours," he said to himself.

Later, Dad had to sew on a button, but he couldn't thread the needle.

"Here, you do it, Biff," he said. "You've got sharp eyes."

"What's all that smoke?" said Anna.

Everyone ran into the kitchen. Smoke was coming out of the oven. Oh no! Dad's cake was burned.

"It says gas mark 3, not 8," said Biff. "It's cinder cake, not carrot cake. Oh Dad, you need to get your eyes tested, too!"

Talk about the story

How did the strawberry sauce get on to the pizza?

Why did Mum and Kipper go to the optician?

What did the optician tell Kipper to do?

If things looked fuzzy to you, who would you tell?

How to look after your eyes

Do

Sit up nice and straight
when you're reading,
writing or drawing.

Wear sunglasses
when you are in
strong sunshine.

Have your eyes
tested regularly.

Tell a grown up if you
get headaches or things
look fuzzy.

Don't

Hold your book too close when you're reading.

Put your nose on the desk when you're writing or drawing.

Look directly at the sun.

Shine lights in anyone's eyes.

Why is it important to look after your eyes?

Which glasses?

Match the right glasses to the six people

Have you read them all yet?

Kipper's First Pet

Learning to Swim

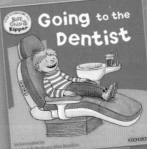

Going to the Dentist

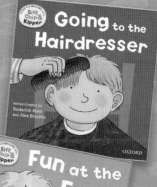

Going to the Hairdresser

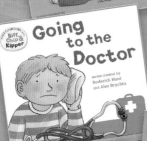

Going to the Doctor

Going on a Plane

Let's Recycle!

Fun at the Farm

Kipper Gets Nits

Going to the Hospital

Going to the Optician

Starting School

FIRST EXPERIENCES Flashcards
55 cards

Kipper's First Dance Class

A New Baby

Kipper's First Match

Going to the Vet

Read with Biff, Chip and Kipper
The UK's best-selling home reading series

Phonics

First Stories

	Phonics				First Stories			
Level 1 Getting ready to read	Kipper's Alphabet I Spy	Chip's Letter Sounds	Biff's Wonder Words	Floppy's Fun Phonics	Get On	Floppy Did This!	Up You Go	Six in a Bed
Level 2 Starting to read	I am Kipper	Cat in a Bag	The Red Hen	The Fizz-Buzz	Funny Fish	Silly Races!	The Snowman	Dad's Birthday
Level 3 Becoming a reader	Such a Fuss	Shops	The Sing Song	The Backpack	Poor Old Rabbit	I Can Trick a Tiger	Super Dad	Floppy and the Bone
Level 4 Developing as a reader	Wet Feet	The Moon Jet	The Red Coat	Quick! Quick!	Missing!	The Raft Race	Dragon Danger	The Spaceship
Level 5 Building confidence in reading	Egg Fried Rice	Craig Saves the Day	Seasick	Dolphin Rescue	Hungry Floppy	Husky Adventure	Trapped!	Looking after Gran
Level 6 Reading with confidence	Gran's New Blue Shoes	Ice City	Save Pudding Wood	Uncle Max	Hairy-Scary Monster	Mountain Rescue	The Lost Voice	Secret of the Sands

Phonics stories help children practise their sounds and letters, as they learn to do in school.

First Stories have been specially written to provide practice in reading everyday language.

READ WITH Biff, Chip & Kipper

OXFORD
UNIVERSITY PRESS

Great Clarendon Street, Oxford OX2 6DP

Text © Roderick Hunt and Annemarie Young 2009
Illustrations © Alex Brychta 2009
First published 2009
This edition published 2014

10 9 8 7 6 5 4 3 2 1
Series Editors: Kate Ruttle, Annemarie Young
British Library Cataloguing in Publication Data available
ISBN: 978-0-19-273680-2
Printed in China by Imago
The characters in this work are the original creation of Roderick Hunt and Alex Brychta who retain copyright in the characters
With thanks to Alison Lask, MCOptom BSc Hons and Dr Veronica Spooner.